ARMEL'S REVENGE

For all those who welcome strangers
into their midst.

First published in Great Britain in 2011 and in the USA in 2012 by
Frances Lincoln Children's Books, 4 Torriano Mews,
Torriano Avenue, London NW5 2RZ
www.franceslincoln.com

A catalogue record for this book is available from the British Library.

ISBN 978-1-84780-224-8

Set in Bembo

Printed and bound by CPI Group (UK) Ltd, Croydon CR0 4YY. in September 2011

1 3 5 7 9 8 6 4 2

ARMEL'S REVENGE

Nicki Cornwell

Illustrated by
Erika Pal

F
FRANCES LINCOLN
CHILDREN'S BOOKS

The New Kid

Christophe looked up as the classroom door opened and in came Mrs Thompson, the Head of Year. She was followed by a thickset, scowling boy with powerful shoulders and solid, scarred hands, who glared round at the waiting class. For a moment he locked eyes with Christophe, then he lowered his eyes to the floor.

"I would not want to fight with *him*!" mouthed Con.

There was something about the way that the boy had looked at Christophe that made him feel uneasy. After exchanging a few words with their teacher, Miss Nagi, Mrs Thompson went out, leaving the new boy behind.

"This is Armel," Miss Nagi. "He's from the Congo, which is a country in Africa. Con, will you move over to that empty desk, please?

I'm going to put Armel next to Christophe because they can both speak French."

Con's face dropped. Obediently he gathered up his books and changed desks. Christophe felt a stab of dismay. There was no way he wanted to sit next to this sulky, glowering boy.

Armel shambled over the floor, and took his place by Christophe. He glared round at the watching kids, as if to push their inquisitive eyes away, then he folded his arms and stared at the desk.

"You'll help Armel, won't you, Christophe?" Miss Nagi pleaded with a smile. "He doesn't speak any English yet, but he'll soon pick it up."

Christophe bit his lip and squashed back his disappointment. He had not forgotten the day he started school four years ago, after his long journey from Rwanda. Never before had he felt so lonely. He had hung about in the playground, wishing someone would talk to him, and then one day they had invited him to

play football. After that he had stopped feeling so scared. He felt sorry for Armel. Naggy meant well. She was trying to help him.

Miss Nagi said, "Will you explain to Armel that he has to stay with you?"

Christophe turned to Armel and said, "*Je m'appelle Christophe. Miss Nagi veut que tu restes avec moi, pour que tu ne te perdes pas.*"

Armel gave a sullen shrug, otherwise there was no sign that he had understood what Christophe said. He kept his eyes on the desk.

"Thank you, Christophe," said Miss Nagi, giving Christophe a smile that was far too bright. She made her way to the front of the class and clapped her hands. "Pay attention, everyone, please!"

The lesson began. While Miss Nagi was talking, Christophe shot a sideways look at the new boy. He wasn't as tall as Christophe, and his skin was darker, but he was much more solidly built. The fact that he was not in school uniform had the effect of making him look older than the others in the class. Everything about him – the way he sat, the way he hunched his shoulders and screwed up his face – told Christophe that Armel did not like school and did not want to be there.

Con flashed Christophe a grin that said, *What bad luck to get dumped with someone like that*. Christophe pulled a face in agreement.

◇ ◇ ◇

That was the beginning of a very bad day. Armel greeted everything that Christophe said with the same sullen, glowering expression. At break, he rose to his feet with surly reluctance and followed Christophe out to the playground. Con hung around briefly, but was driven away by Armel's scowl, and the impossibility of communicating with him.

Dismayed at Con's desertion, Christophe began to wish that a hole in the ground would open up and Armel would fall into it. Quite without realising what he was doing, he slipped his hand into his shirt and ran his fingers over the scar on the side of his body. This was something that he automatically did when he felt uncertain and in need of comfort.

Touching his scar brought back the memory of the day he had fallen over in the playground in his primary school. He had winded himself, and Greg had lifted up his shirt and seen his scar. How the kids had stared! They had cried out, "What's that?" "How did you get it?" and Christophe had scowled at them the way Armel was scowling now.

He had wanted to push them away, he wanted them to stop staring, but somehow he had managed to tell the others about the bad things that had happened in Rwanda, and why he now had a scar. They had been fascinated; they had hung about him like dogs waiting to be fed, and he had not wanted to stop talking. After that, he had felt a lot better. Maybe there was a story that Armel did not want to tell, maybe Armel had scars that he kept hidden?

But Armel was like a bomb that might explode; it was not safe to ask questions.

Christophe decided to try talking about the teachers and the school instead, but Armel slouched against the wall with a bored frown, and Christophe struggled to find words. At last the bell rang for the end of break.

"You dumped me in it," he hissed at Con as they went into the classroom. "Why didn't you stick around?"

Con spread his hands. "I couldn't talk to him!"

"Nor could I," fumed Christophe.

"Tell you what, I'll see if Hitch has got his cards for the dinner break," Con offered.

When the lunch-time break came, Christophe went out into the playground, shadowed by a silent Armel. Con and Hitch were waiting by the bollard with the flat top on which they played cards. Hitch waved the pack at Christophe and Armel and said, "Play cards?"

Armel shook his head. Christophe felt like a drowning man who had been thrown a line only to have it snatched away from him. In a split-second of fury he decided that he had had enough. He had done his best. "You can watch, then," he shrugged.

Con shuffled, Hitch dealt, and the game began. Around them were the shouts and scuffles of the playground, of kids letting off steam after being cooped up in class. Absorbed in their game, oblivious to the noise, they played on. Christophe was winning; he had good cards and he was playing them well. But at the last minute Hitch scooped a victory.

The bell rang. Hastily they scooped up the cards and Hitch put them away in his pocket. Only then did Christophe remember the new boy. He looked round, his stomach began to knot up.

"Where's Armel?" he cried.

"Gone to the loo?" Con suggested.

"I'm supposed to look after him!"

"He's not a baby, he can manage," said Hitch. "Come on, Naggy will have a go at us if we're late."

Christophe followed Hitch back to the classroom, but he couldn't stop his stomach churning with worry. With a sinking heart he saw that the new boy's desk was empty.

"Where's Armel?" said Miss Nagi with concern.

"He was watching us play cards. Then he wasn't there. I don't know where he went," said Christophe.

Miss Nagi pursed her lips. "You were supposed to be looking after him, Christophe. We must let the office know that he's missing. You can do that on your way to your next lesson. Off you go, all of you, the first years are waiting to come in."

By the time Christophe had finished telling the secretary in the office what had happened, and explaining to the History teacher why he was late, his cheeks were burning with shame.

"Wasn't your fault, Chris," Con said kindly as they walked back home.

"Was," Christophe answered gloomily.

◊   ◊   ◊

"You coming in?" said Con.

"Yeah, why not?"

Christophe and Con had been friends ever since the start of secondary school, and Christophe often stopped at Con's house on the way back home. Con was small and wiry, gentle and funny. He had a big sister, Kathleen, who had just left school, and twin brothers called Declan and Ciarán, and he lived in a house that was full of warmth and noise and clutter. The television was always on, but no one ever watched it. Deirdre, his mum, was small and kind and wired up with tension. She was forever baking, while the twins rattled round the house fighting and yelling at each other, and Kathleen sat watching everything with her knowing green eyes. Christophe was both fascinated and confused by Kathleen; she had an answer for everything.

Con and Christophe had only just sat down at the kitchen table when the twins erupted into the room.

"You broke it!"

"I did not!"

"You did so!"

Deirdre said wearily, "Will youse two stop getting at each other?"

"Ciarán started it!"

"No I didn't!"

"Did!"

"Didn't!"

Kathleen reached out an arm and caught hold of Declan. "You heard what Mam said. Be quiet!" Seizing the chance, Ciarán darted out of the room.

"Leggo!" shrieked Declan. "I'm going to get him!"

"Go on, then," said Kath, letting go of him. "Beat the living daylights out of each other if you must. See if I care."

"They're as bad as the Prods and the Papists, so they are," grumbled Deirdre. "They wouldn't be like that if their daddy was here."

"Want to bet?" said Kath with a grin. She slid her long, slim body from her chair. "I must be off; I've my homework to do."

"Homework?" said Christophe. "I thought you left school?"

"I'm at the hairdressers, aren't I? And I'm at college two days a week. School doesn't stop if you want to get on in life," said Kath.

She threw a smile to Christophe and left the room. Christophe felt as if the sun had come out, and all too soon had gone in again.

◇ ◇ ◇

"How was school?" Christophe's mother, Mbika, asked.

"All right. When's Papa coming home?"

"Soon. That's if the clinic doesn't go on late."

Christophe's father was working as a

doctor in the local hospital. In Rwanda, André had been a hospital consultant, but when he and his family came to the UK as asylum-seekers neither he nor Mbika were allowed to work. Three years later, they were at last accepted as refugees, and André had wasted no time in finding a job.

In the living room, Christophe's little sister Alisha was colouring in pictures. Briefly looking up, she said, "I'm colouring."

"Why?" Christophe asked. *Why* was Alisha's favourite word, and he said it to tease her.

"Because I want to."

Christophe sank on to the sofa and listened to the stillness of the room, a silence only broken by Alisha's pencil marking the page. How different it was from Con's house, where people, animals, and everything around them merged into a muddle, and no one could hear themselves think. Here in the flat, where everything was tidy and in its place, and Papa and Maman, Alisha and himself all had their separate spaces, he could listen to his mind.

What was wrong with that new boy? Why did he behave the way he did?

Later, Christophe told his parents how Naggy had told him to look after Armel. "She made him sit by me because he doesn't speak any English. I was supposed to look after him, but I couldn't find him because he walked out of school and he didn't come back."

"I hope no one bullied him," said Mbika.

"He's not that kind of boy."

"Which country has he come from?" asked Papa.

"The Congo."

"He'll be an asylum-seeker," said Papa with a sigh. "He'll have a story to tell, poor kid."

Mbika frowned. "Some stories are better not told."

"Why?" asked Alisha.

"Because they're bad stories."

"Why?"

"They make you sad."

"*Snow White* make me sad, then I happy again," observed Alisha.

"Time to get ready for bed," said Mbika.

◇ ◇ ◇

"You're home early!" exclaimed Armel's mother, Kwayera. She spoke in French. "What happened? What's wrong?"

"I walked out of school," scowled Armel.

"Why?"

"They put me next to an *inyenzi*!"

Kwayera caught her breath. "How do you know?"

"You only have to look at him."

Kwayera sat down. Her face went pale. "What did he do?"

"Nothing," snapped Armel. "And he's not going to do anything, either."

"Keep away from him," Kwayera said sharply.

Resentment swelled up in Armel. "Why do I have to go to school? I'm too old for school. I did a man's work before, didn't I?"

Kwayera gave a stifled cry. She fled into her bedroom and slammed the door shut.

Armel stormed off to his own bedroom

and threw himself on his bed. That was what his mother always did. She shut him up, just as surely as she had slammed that door. The awful events of the past lay inside him like a piece of bad meat that he had swallowed and he could not digest. If only he could talk to someone about the things that had happened! A wave of pain rose up inside him. He punched the pillow and thumped the wall, but nothing drove away the pain.

Christophe breathed a sigh of relief when Armel failed to arrive at school the next day. Con asked if he could sit by Christophe again, but Miss Nagi refused his request. Christophe and Con exchanged glances.

"That means he'll be back," said Christophe gloomily.

"Bad luck!" Con sympathised.

Armel returns to school

Two days later Armel waited with his mother outside the Head of Year's room. A dull hard feeling sat in his chest, weighing him down.

The day after he had walked out of school, two men had come round to the flat. One was a teacher, the other an interpreter. They had spoken in French. They used words as weapons; they were like vultures circling round for the kill. Kwayera had been shaken and upset. Armel wanted to lash out at them, but he knew it was no use doing so. He had to sit on his hands to hold his anger back when Kwayera promised that they would both go to see the Head of Year the following morning.

After they had gone, Kwayera had said angrily, "You heard that? They will give me trouble if you don't go to school. That's the way it is here."

"That's stupid," Armel said sullenly.

"Stupid or not, you'll have to go."

"I'm not a kid. I did what the men did, didn't I?"

Kwayera turned on him, eyes blazing with fury. "Enough of that! You must go to school. Do you want us to get kicked out of the country?"

Armel bit his lip. He was responsible for his mother; he had promised his brother Laurent he would take care of her. He would go back to school, he would learn this dull, heavy language whose words dropped out of the mouths of the speakers and fell on the floor like stones. He would show them what he could do, even if it meant going back to being a kid once more.

"Very well."

"Keep away from the *inyenzi,* you hear me?"

Armel made no answer. Somehow, he did not know how, he was going to revenge himself on the *inyenzi* for the things that the cockroaches had done to his family.

"You hear me?" Kwayera repeated sharply.

"I hear you." That was not a promise, was it?

Later that day they went out to the shops to buy school uniform with the coupons that Kwayera had been given. Armel tried on the uniform and stared at himself in the mirror in disbelief. Instead of a man, he saw a young, lost boy. And when they set off for the school on the following day, and he was wearing his new school uniform, he felt as if he had shrunk back into being a kid, and it was all he could do to keep his head held high.

◇ ◇ ◇

An interpreter arrived, and they all went in. Miss Nagi was waiting with Mrs Thompson. She smiled at Armel, but there was no way he would return the smile. The interview began. All the words that were said had to travel from English into French and from French into English; this was a long, slow journey.

Mrs Thompson began by asking Armel what had happened to make him walk out of school.

"Nothing," shrugged Armel.

"Did anyone treat you badly?"

"No."

"Then why did you walk out?"

Armel felt fury gathering up in his head, like a storm about to break. Words were rushing round in his head like animals in a cage. He closed his mouth and he kept it shut.

Mrs Thompson asked Armel's mother if she could throw any light on what had gone on. Kwayera responded angrily, quickly. Her hands jabbed the air.

The interpreter said, "She says that Armel thinks that he is too old for school."

"Too old?" said Mrs Thompson, with a puzzled expression.

A rapid outburst of words shot from Kwayera's mouth. She spoke in French. "It's different where I come from. You don't go to school at his age because there isn't one.

He left school a couple of years ago, and since then he's been doing a man's work. How else would we all survive? If you don't grow what you can, you've got nothing to eat. And then there's the war. . ."

Armel felt a rising fury. He could see the clouds in his mother's eyes, he could feel the anger forcing her words out. Images of the holes that he had dug, of the bodies that were waiting, floated into his head. He dug his nails into his hand to push them away. These people were all so stupid, they understood nothing.

"He hasn't been to school for a year or so," the interpreter reported to Mrs Thompson. "And then she started talking about the war, but she didn't seem to want to go into that."

"I see," said Mrs Thompson doubtfully. "Tell her that in this country it's compulsory for young people of his age to attend school. Does she understand that?"

The interpreter spoke to Kwayera; Kwayera nodded.

"Very well. I shall allow Armel to rejoin his class," said Mrs Thompson.

Armel walked with Miss Nagi down the corridor to the classroom. He tried to imagine that he was being escorted to a detention camp by a soldier, but he didn't feel like a man. He had reverted to being a helpless child.

◇　◇　◇

Christophe's heart sank when Armel marched into the classroom and sat down by him. Armel seemed calmer, but there was something dangerous about the calm that Christophe distrusted.

"*Dis-lui que je ne veux pas m'asseoir à côté de toi. Je ne veux pas parler francais, je veux apprendre à parler l'anglais,*" he hissed out of the side of his mouth.

"Armel says he doesn't want to sit by me. He doesn't want to speak French, he wants to learn English," Christophe reported to Miss Nagi.

Naggy inclined her head and told Armel and Conor to swap desks. So now Con was sitting by Christophe again, and Christophe was free of responsibility for Armel. This was a relief, but there was something about the way that Armel was determined *not* to look at Christophe that made him uncomfortable. He felt threatened by the new boy's presence and he was unable to understand why.

"You know what?" said Con when they were playing cards in the break. "That new kid spooks me."

"Me too," said Hitch. "He grabs hold of you and points at something and he says, 'What is?' You give him the word, you don't dare not. No one likes him."

"He blanks you, Chris, doesn't he?" said Con. "Why's that?"

"Dunno," said Christophe shortly. "Your turn to deal."

◇ ◇ ◇

Papa was at home when Christophe got back from school. He was reading a newspaper. He looked up as Christophe entered the room – a storm was raging in his face.

"What is it?" cried Christophe.

"Something I was reading," said Papa with an effort. The fire in his eyes was dying down, the storm was easing. He was forcing the thing that he had read out of his mind. That was what Papa always did when something upset him. He put the newspaper down, and as he did so, Christophe caught sight of the word *RWANDA*. He made up his mind to read the paper when Papa had laid it aside, and find out what had upset his father.

"Guess what?" he said. "The new boy came back, but he's not sitting by me any more. He doesn't want to speak French, he wants to learn English."

"That's good," Papa said.

"Where's Maman?"

"At the shops with Alisha. She won't be long."

Later that evening Christophe searched for the newspaper that had set Papa's eyes on fire, but it was nowhere to be found.

◇ ◇ ◇

"How was school?" said Kwayera. Anxiety made her voice harsh.

"I made the teacher move me away from the *inyenzi*," Armel said. "I don't want to have anything to do with him."

"Wherever there's an *inyenzi* there's trouble," said Kwayera. The scar on her cheek trembled as her face quivered. "Put your coat on again, I want you to come shopping with me. I don't understand a word they say."

"It's raining," grumbled Armel as he pulled on his jacket.

It was always raining. Not thick, heavy rain that poured down from the sky and flooded the earth, but a thin, misting rain that gradually soaked into the clothes that he wore and chilled his bones. And if the sun came out, it was a watered down sun that wasn't powerful enough to dry things out.

"Stupid country, stupid language," he grumbled to himself.

The Poison of the Past

Some weeks later, Christophe was lining up outside a classroom with the other children when Con said, "I saw Armel coming out of Westwood House."

"Yeah?"

"He was with his mum. She's got a scar on one side of her face, like a pirate. And she walks funny – she's got a bad leg."

"Yeah?"

"He's still blanking you, isn't he?"

"Yeah."

"I don't like him."

"Me neither."

The teacher was late arriving. The line had broken up; the children were milling around. They were only just keeping their voices down. Suddenly, Christophe felt himself shoved to one side. He looked round – it was Armel.

"*Inyenzi*!" hissed Armel. Christophe shrank back, such was the revulsion in Armel's voice. He felt his fingers curl into fists, ready to defend himself, but Armel backed off and turned away.

"What was all that about?" cried Con.

"Dunno."

"Was that a swear word? That *yenzi* thing he said?"

"No idea."

Shaken by the hatred that he had seen in Armel's eyes, the word "*inyenzi*" lodged itself in Christophe's brain as if it were the key to a puzzle that he had always known existed, but he had only just recognised.

◇ ◇ ◇

"What does *inyenzi* mean?" he asked his father. "Is it a swear word?"

Papa's head shot up. "Who said that to you?"

"Armel did."

"What happened?" Papa asked sharply.

Taken aback by the urgency in his father's voice, Christophe said, "Nothing! I thought he was going to hit me, but he backed off. What does that word mean?"

André's eyes clouded over. His voice sounded as if the words were being dragged out of him. "It's a Kinyarwandan word for an insect that you find back home. In English you call it a cockroach."

As he was speaking, Mbika came into the room. Her hand flew up to her lips, she gave an exclamation of horror. André jerked up from the computer and she buried her head in his shoulder; she was shaking soundlessly.

"What's the matter?" cried Christophe. "What have I done?"

"Nothing, Christophe," André said wretchedly. "You've done nothing wrong."

"I don't want to talk about it!" Mbika cried. She spoke in French, she always used French when she was upset.

André answered in the same language. "We knew this would happen one day, we knew he'd ask. We have to tell him."

"I suppose so." Mbika's voice was small, muffled by Andre's shoulder. Christophe felt his stomach tighten. Maman was upset, badly upset.

"You could go to the park with Alisha, while Christophe and I talk?"

"Yes, I'll do that."

Mbika raised her head. Her face was like a stone, dull and flat. Without once looking at Christophe, she turned away and left the room. The sound of her voice could be heard, calling to Alisha. Then the front door shut, and Christophe was alone with Papa.

◇　◇　◇

"I don't want to talk about this any more than Maman does," said Papa, "But the story must be told. Sit down on the sofa by me." His voice was rough; he cleared his throat. "I can't tell it in English, I must tell it in French."

Christophe sank down beside his father. "You don't have to tell me."

Papa shook his head. "It's not good to make a mystery of the past. If you do that it's impossible to face the facts. You know that story of yours, the one your teacher helped you to write?"

"Yes."

"You told the story when you were eight, but you were six when it all happened. When you had to run away with Maman and go to live with Babi. You remember?"

"Babi used to tell me stories. And I went out on the hills with the goats," smiled Christophe. Then his smile dropped. "Maman was there, but you didn't come. I didn't see you for a long time."

The warm image of Babi faded; in its place came the memory of men bursting into the house, with chalk marks over their faces, drums banging, fear rising. Maman had shrunk back, Papa had gone with them. Matthieu had started to cry – Matthieu, his little brother, who wasn't there any more.

"You went off with them," he accused

Papa. "You didn't argue with them. I knew they were bad men. I was scared."

"I was scared too," Papa said. "I had to act like they were my friends. If I had argued with them they would have killed me. They would have killed all of us."

Papa had been scared? Christophe felt cold with fear. "Wh . . . what did they want you to do?"

"They wanted me put Hutu patients first and ignore the Tutsis. I'm a doctor; a doctor should treat all patients equally. I couldn't do that." Papa's voice was harsh, he was upset.

"Hutus? Tutsis? What are you talking about?"

"Hutu is one kind of Rwandan, Tutsi is another. I'm a Hutu. So are you."

"Am I?"

"If your father is Hutu, you are Hutu. If he's Tutsi, you are Tutsi."

Christophe's head felt heavy and confused. He was struggling to understand. He searched his memory; pictures came flooding back.

Papa had gone, they had nothing to eat. Mama crying, Matthieu crying. The drums, the bad men coming back. Running, running with Maman, Matthieu on her back. Shooting. The house going up in flames.

"The bad men came back and set fire to the house."

"That's right," said Papa.

"Why? Was it because you wouldn't do what they wanted?"

"No. It was because Maman is a Tutsi."

"She can't be!"

"Her father was Tutsi and so she is Tutsi too. That's why she's so tall and slim. And you take after her. You are Hutu, but you look like a Tutsi," Papa said.

"I look like a Tutsi?" Christophe felt as if the room was swimming round him. The floor was dancing up and down. A sharp pain stabbed his chest. How could Papa and Maman be two different things? And what was he, Christophe, if he was part of one and part of the other?

"Yes. You are tall and slim, not short and fat like me. And your skin is paler, just like Maman's." Papa was trying to make a joke of it, but Christophe knew that he wasn't really joking. His voice was tight and unhappy.

"That is why Armel called you an *inyenzi*. He thinks you're a Tutsi."

Christophe felt his chest grow tight. He had to force out his voice. "What is wrong with being Tutsi?"

"Nothing – and everything," André said heavily. "I'll try to explain. You are the storyteller now that Babi has gone, but today it's my turn to tell you a story. A story about the poison of the past."

Papa's Story

"Long ago," said André, "Hutus and Tutsis lived side by side in Rwanda. They were friendly, they didn't hate each other the way they do now. But that was before the Europeans took over the country. People came from France and later from Belgium. Teachers came, there were more schools in Rwanda, but the lessons were in French, not in Kinyarwanda. We Rwandans were bought with their money and their knowledge."

Christophe wriggled uneasily. "You said you were going to tell me a story. This isn't a story, it's a History lesson," he protested.

"History is stories about things that happened in the past," André said. "I'm talking about the time that *my* babi was a little boy."

"My babi's papa?"

"That's right. And this is Rwandan

history. What happened in Rwanda is part of European history too, but perhaps the Europeans would rather not remember that."

"Why?"

"Listen to the story and you'll see why."

André pulled out a handkerchief and wiped the sweat from his forehead. Then he continued, "Once the Europeans were in control of Rwanda, they gave the best jobs to the Tutsis. That's called 'divide and rule'. You give power to one group so that the two groups won't gang up against you. But that made a lot of trouble because there were far more Hutus than Tutsis."

"Then why didn't they make the Hutus the bosses?"

"Because those Europeans had poison in their heads and they poisoned the heads of the Africans. They chose the Tutsis because their skin was paler than the Hutus and they looked more *European*; they thought that must mean that the Tutsis were more intelligent than the Hutus."

"That's racism, isn't it?" said Christophe.

"Yes."

"We've learned about that at school. You're not allowed to insult anyone because of their colour."

"That's right, but you have to remember that what is said and done now isn't what was said and done in the past. And what is said and done in one country is often different from another. And this is what happened in Rwanda. Some Tutsis began to believe they were superior to Hutus because they got chosen for the best jobs; and many of the Hutus began to think that they must be more stupid than the Tutsis. That was the poison at work."

"Was your head poisoned too?"

"Yes," said André, "till I started to work things out for myself. You mustn't believe all that your parents tell you – or your teachers, for that matter. People often believe things that aren't correct. They think they know, but what they know is the lies they've been told."

"Lies?" Christophe asked.

"Lies, stories — what's the difference?" André said impatiently. "We all tell stories about the past and we've all got different stories. One man's story is another man's lie. Let me get on with what I have to say."

Papa's voice had deepened; there were clouds in his eyes. Christophe began to feel scared. Papa must be coming to the bad bit, the bit that Maman had not wanted him to hear.

"When the Europeans pulled out of Rwanda they left the Tutsis in charge. People were poor, people were hungry. The Hutus said there were far more Hutus than Tutsis, and that they ought to be in control. And the rumblings and grumblings went on, until one day the Hutus turned on the Tutsis. That was what happened when you were six."

Papa's eyes were wet with tears. Christophe slid his hand into Papa's and held on tight.

Papa said, "They said the Tutsi were cockroaches. 'Kill the *inyenzi*,' they said, 'Kill

the cockroaches.' The Hutus started killing and they didn't stop. The killing went on and on."

Christophe felt as if the breath had been knocked out of him. "Didn't anyone stop them?"

"Nobody did," Papa said bitterly. "The only people who could have stopped them were the foreigners, but they didn't do anything. They got out and left the killing to go on. It was genocide, that's what it was, and they didn't intervene."

"Genocide?" Christophe's memory flickered into life. "That's what Hitler did to the Jews, isn't it?"

He had read about the Nazis and concentration camps in a book. They had talked about it in a History lesson. All the kids had said how horrible that was, and one of them had had to go out and be sick. But that had happened a long time ago in another country, and it had happened in the past. And now Papa was saying that something like that had happened in Rwanda and it had happened when Christophe was six. Christophe felt dizzy with fear. His head was spinning like a top.

"Yes, it was genocide," André said. "If you looked like a Tutsi, you had had it, and if you stuck up for a Tutsi you were in deep trouble. I stuck up for the Tutsis. That's why they wanted me to go with them. To put pressure on me."

A fleeting memory came back to Christophe of the little brother that he had played with as a child. "Matthieu was shot, wasn't he?"

"That's right," Papa said dully. His grip tightened.

"I was shot too," said Christophe. He put his hand inside his shirt and fingered the long, lumpy scar left by the bullet that had grazed him.

"You are lucky to be alive."

"And then I was ill and I woke up in Babi's house," said Christophe.

"You had a fever," said Papa. "The wound was infected."

"And Babi gave me something horrible to drink, and I got better. And then you sent for us, and we came to this country." Words tumbled out of his mouth, anything to stop Papa being so sad. "And I had to learn English. And we were asylum-seekers but now we're refugees. We can stay here now, we can't be sent back to Rwanda. And you're a doctor again."

"And you have a little sister," said Papa.

"Maybe I'll have another little brother!"

"Maybe," said Papa.

Papa was making an effort to smile. That was better, but good stories get back to the beginning before they come to an end, and the story had begun with Armel. There was one more question Christophe had to ask.

"How does Armel know about cockroaches?"

The smile fell from Papa's face. "He's probably a Hutu whose family have fled from the Congo. The poison from the past has spread; the infection has reached other countries."

"What if I tell him what you've told me? Wouldn't that help?"

"I doubt it. Armel will have his own story to tell. Keep away from that boy, he can do you no good. This poison is strong, it makes people burn with anger and turn against each other."

"Isn't there a way of stopping the poison?"

"Not that I know of. I read in the paper that there's a possibility that the Belgian Prime Minister might apologise for pulling the troops out of the country and letting the Hutus get on with it, but what does that do for anyone?"

"You told me that saying 'sorry' helps!" protested Christophe.

"Yes, it can; if the wrongdoer feels remorse and apologises to the person he has wronged," said André. "But how can someone who wasn't there apologise for what happened? And how can it help people who are dead? How can a person who has suffered not be angry?"

Papa usually had an answer for everything, but this time it seemed that Papa had run out of them. Suddenly Christophe remembered something that Papa had said some time ago.

'You remember how I was angry with those kids who bullied me? And how I wanted to hurt them?'

"Yes?"

"You told me it's important to forgive?"

Papa nodded. "That's right."

"Then you should forgive the Belgians, shouldn't you?"

"I suppose so." Papa's smile was wry.

"And the Hutus?"

A quiver passed over Papa's face. "You're right," he conceded sadly. "I should try. How else can I draw a line under the past? But I don't find it easy. Maman and I don't talk about these things. Maybe deep down inside us the poison is still causing us harm. And we didn't want to talk about it to you, we were afraid that you would be infected by it. Beware of the poison of the past, Christophe, try not to get infected."

"I'll try," Christophe promised.

◇ ◇ ◇

But as Christophe lay in bed that night, his head was churning with the story that Papa had told him. The story that he had told in his primary school, the one that the teacher had taken down and made into a book, was only part of a story. Much, much more had happened in Rwanda than he had realised. Babi was right, stories should not be written down. Once they were written, they could not be changed. Papa's story was richer and deeper than the story that he had told the kids in his primary school. And what did Papa mean by saying that Armel would have his own story?

And then there was this new consciousness of himself – that his father was Hutu and his mother was Tutsi, and he, Christophe, was both. Yet Hutus thought of Tutsis as insects, they had hated them enough to kill them. He had always thought that it was soldiers who had shot at him and burned down the house, but now that Christophe knew that these things had been done by Hutus, it was as if one part of himself was at war with the other.

A wave of sadness threatened to engulf him. He pushed the feeling away. Why should he feel sad for something that happened so long ago? How dare the Hutus shoot at him, how dare they kill Matthieu? He felt long, cold tendrils of anger curling round his heart, as if a nest of snakes had lodged inside him.

Armel had better not call him an *inyenzi* again!

◆ ◆ ◆

A watery sun was sinking in the sky as Christophe and Con walked back from school together.

"Armel has got it in for you," Con said knowingly.

"Yeah."

"Why's that?"

Christophe was reluctant to talk about the story that Papa had told him, but somehow Con dragged it out of him.

"Let me get this right. Your dad and mum look different from each other," Con said. "One's a Two-two and the other's a Tootsi?"

"Hutu and Tutsi," said Christophe.

"And your mum's lot were on top, so your dad's lot started killing your mum's lot?"

"Yeah."

"And you and Armel are both Who-twos, but you look like your mum, so Armel thinks you're a Tootsi and that's why he hates you?"

Christophe gave an unhappy nod. "My dad says it's poison that comes from the past."

"Yeah, well, that's like us," said Con gloomily. "My mam's family were on one side and my da's on the other. He went back to Ireland to see his people and got blown up by a bomb, and it was my mam's side that did it."

"How old were you?"

"I was seven. Kath was ten and the twins were babies."

"The Hutus killed my little brother," said Christophe. "Wasn't soldiers that did it, it was Hutus."

"Yeah, but it wasn't Armel's fault, was it?"

"S'pose not."

"Coming in?"

Christophe shook his head. "Not tonight. I've got to go home."

He did not want to sit down in the muddle and noise of Con's house, not when there was so much that he had to think about. Now he knew what had happened to Con's father, he felt very sorry for Con. And he could not help thinking about what it would have been like if the Hutus had killed Papa.

The Fight

In the days that followed, Christophe became increasingly annoyed by Armel's efforts to blank him. What right did Armel have to behave like that, after all that the Hutus had done to the Tutsis? He longed to avenge himself on Armel, yet his father's words echoed in his ears.

"Beware of the poison of the past, try not to get infected."

And even as he tried to fight against infection, he remembered his little brother, Matthieu, who had been killed by the Hutus. The fire of injustice burned inside him and the flames were fanned by his anger. Sometimes he stared long and hard at Armel, at other times he acted cool and blanked him back. The poison had taken hold of him.

Armel, for his part, was consumed by

hatred for Christophe. After the *inyenzi* had done what they did, Laurent had gone in search of revenge, but Armel, the younger brother, had been forced to stay behind to look after their mother. Chance had thrown an *inyenzi* in his path, and sooner or later there would be an opportunity to take his own revenge. Not in school, where everyone would see what was happening, but outside. Meanwhile, he made himself attend school and drove himself to learn English. He blanked the *inyenzi* and he forced himself to listen to the teachers, but he was always conscious of the *inyenzi's* presence. Hatred smouldered inside him, waiting for the chance to break out into fire.

At school Christophe and Armel were forced to be in the same room with each other most of the day. The atmosphere between them was like a thunderstorm building up. The children who noticed what was going on were careful to avoid triggering the storm. They avoided Christophe as much as they did Armel.

"Is anything wrong between you and Armel?" Miss Nagi asked Christophe.

Christophe clammed up. "No."

"Have you had an argument?"

"No, miss."

◇ ◇ ◇

A few weeks later, Armel and Christophe came face to face one Saturday morning. Armel was out on an erand for his mother when the *inyenzi* emerged from a side alley. Armel jerked to a halt. The *inyenzi* froze, paralysed with fear. No one else was about. The street was deserted; here was a chance for revenge. Armel let loose a cry of rage. "*Inyenzi!*"

He bunched his hands into fists, ready to lash out, but it was too late. The *inyenzi* had shot back into the alley, and Armel's fist hit the wall. Knuckles bleeding and full of fury, Armel pounded down the passage in pursuit.

◇ ◇ ◇

Sick with panic, Christophe hurtled between the narrow walls of the passage. Fighting was not an option, not when faced with an adversary as powerful as Armel. He had his precious mobile in his pocket, but there was no way he could summon help. Footsteps thudded after him; how could he get away?

And then he remembered that on the other side of the wall there was an abandoned building site that he knew well – he and Con had often played football among the rubble and the bushes. If he could scale the wall before Armel caught hold of him, he could drop down on the other side and escape through the entrance.

Halfway down the alley he leaped at the wall, clambered up it and slithered over, landing with a jolt that shuddered the air out of him. As he fought for breath, he heard the sound of Armel scrabbling up the wall. Just as he got his breath back, Armel's head appeared over the top of the wall.

"*Inyenzi!*" he snarled. He pulled himself

up to his full height and hurled himself at Christophe.

Christophe side-stepped. He had no time to run. Panic gave way to fury. How dare Armel treat him like this? The ground shook as Armel landed with a thud beside him. Christophe balled his hands into fists, and thrashed out at his opponent. Fists met flesh as they lunged at each other. Christophe thought only of winning. He wasn't conscious of bruises or pain.

But there came a moment when Armel delivered a punch to Christophe's eye, a blow so powerful that Christophe lost his balance, staggered back and fell on his bottom. Armel rushed towards him, ready to finish things off, but Christophe twisted sideways, snatched a stick from the ground and lunged out. Armel grabbed hold of the stick and tried to wrest it from his opponent's grasp, but Christophe held on with grim determination. Armel changed tactics, he yanked the stick towards him with such force that Christophe was pulled off his feet. Like a bullet from a gun, Christophe flew through the air and smacked into Armel, who fell backwards to the ground with Christophe on top of him. Christophe rolled off. He was about to throw himself at Armel again when he sensed that something was wrong. In the silence of the late afternoon, Armel lay sprawled on the ground, deathly still.

Christophe let out a gasp of horror. He stumbled forward. Blood was coming out of a gash on Armel's head. Christophe fell to his knees and laid his hand on Armel's chest. Armel was still breathing, he wasn't dead and the flow of blood was slowing down. His hair was matted with blood, and there was more on the stone beside him. Armel must have hit it when he fell.

◇ ◇ ◇

Horrified by what had happened, Christophe wanted to turn and run. No one knew that he was there. There was no way he wanted anyone to know about the fight, he did not want to face questions of any kind.

But what would happen to Armel? Maybe he would recover consciousness, get up and go home, but what if he didn't? Armel was hurt, he needed help. Christophe would have to get help, even if by doing so he got himself in trouble.

He took out his mobile. His head throbbed with pain. One of his eyes was closed. He felt sick and panicky and he was unable to think straight. Papa had told him to take the house mobile if he went out by himself so that he could ring for help if he needed it, but who could he phone? Papa's mobile was switched off – he only picked up messages when he had finished work. There was no phone in the flat, so Christophe was unable to ring his mother. The only other number he knew by heart was Con's house phone. He dialled Con's number.

"Hello?" It was Con's voice.

"Con, it's me."

"You sound weird!"

Christophe swallowed. "I need help."

'What's up?"

"Armel's hurt. We had a fight and he fell. He's lying there. He's badly hurt."

"Wait there. I'll get Kath."

Christophe heard Con shouting for Kath. He heard them talking; their voices were high and urgent. Then Kath came onto the phone.

"Christophe, it's me. Armel's hurt?"

"Yes."

"Is he conscious?"

"No. He — he's just lying there."

"I'll call an ambulance. Where are you?"

"On the building site. Near the alley wall. Con knows — he's been here."

"OK. I'll ring you back."

The mobile went dead. Christophe sat waiting. Armel lay without moving. Christophe felt sick and scared. He was shivering with cold. What if Armel were so badly injured that he died? Everyone would think that Christophe was to blame. But Armel had started the fight. Christophe had tried to run away. It wasn't his fault that things had turned out so badly, was it?

Try as he might to convince himself that he was blameless, Christophe knew that there had come a point when he was willing to fight back and he had wanted to hurt Armel. The poison had seeped in to him — he had allowed himself to become infected.

◇ ◇ ◇

At last his mobile rang. Christophe snatched it up.

"The ambulance is on its way," a woman's voice said. "Can I ask you a few questions?"

She asked him about Armel. Where was the wound? How big was it? Was it bleeding? Christophe tried to answer, though he was shaking and his head felt as if it had stopped working. While he was talking to the woman, he heard a shout and Con and Kath came running towards him. Close behind them came the men from the ambulance.

"You all right, Chris?" asked Kath. "Here, take this!"

She pulled off her jacket and wrapped it round him. The jacket smelled of strange scents; it smelled of Kath, Christophe thought. And while this thought was going through his head, he stopped shivering.

Meanwhile the men had checked Armel and wrapped a bandage round his head. They slid a stretcher under his inert body and lifted him up. Then they carried him over the rough ground and loaded him on to the waiting ambulance. Christophe and his friends followed.

"Is he going to be OK?" asked Christophe.

"I hope so," answered one of the men. "Hit his head on that stone, by the looks of it. Lucky you got the ambulance when you did. You're the one that raised the alarm, aren't you?"

"Yes."

"Where are you taking him?" asked Kath.

"The John Cassington."

Kath pointed at Christophe. "That's where his dad works. His dad's a doctor."

"Oh yeah? And what does he think about his son trespassing on private property?"

Christophe hung his head. His cheeks were burning with shame.

"You better get back home and get that eye seen to," said the ambulance man and the ambulance left.

Kath turned to Christophe and said, "You look a mess. Let's get you back home."

◇ ◇ ◇

Mbika gave a wail of dismay. "What's been going on?"

"I got in a fight," said Christophe.

Mbika said nothing more. She cleaned up his face and put a sticky plaster on a cut.

"Does it hurt?" said Alisha.

"A bit," said Christophe.

"Papa will make it better," said his sister with confidence.

◊ ◊ ◊

By the time André got back from work, Christophe was in bed. He heard his father's footsteps coming upstairs and he caught his breath. He was going to have to tell Papa everything that had happened, and he knew that he was going to get told off. He felt sick with misery, and heavy with guilt.

"I hear you've been in a fight," said Papa. "Let's have a look at you."

After Papa had checked Christophe's bruises, he asked Christophe what had happened. Haltingly, Christophe told Papa how he had been running away from Armel and he had scaled the wall into the building site. As soon as he heard this, Papa said, "That wasn't wise. It's safer with other people around."

Christophe hung his head. "I knew the place. I thought I could get away from him there."

"You knew it, did you?" frowned Papa. "You know very well you shouldn't have been there. That's private property!"

"I know."

"I hope it will never happen again, you understand?"

"Yes."

"What happened next?"

"There was a fight," said Christophe. "I fell on the ground, and he grabbed the stick I got hold of, and he tried to get it off me. I held on and I went flying at him and I landed on top of him. And he didn't move, and there was blood on his head, and I knew he needed help. And I called Con. And he got an ambulance and Armel was taken to your hospital."

"I know, I've already seen him."

"Have you?"

"I specialise in Head Injuries, remember? I was right in what I thought, Armel is a Hutu from the Congo. He's lucky you kids got hold of an ambulance. If you'd left him there he'd be in a much worse shape than he is now."

"I didn't mean to hurt him!"

"What do you mean, you didn't mean to hurt him? You were fighting, weren't you?"

"Yes." Christophe hung his head again. "I wanted to run away when I saw him lying there."

"I don't blame you. I doubt if he'd have got an ambulance for you. I'm proud of you, Christophe."

Papa took Christophe by the shoulders and hugged him, and Christophe felt a weight shift from his chest. "Is Armel going to be all right?"

"Maybe, but it's too early to tell. The ward will contact me if anything happens in the night. His mother is with him. Go to sleep now, I'll see you in the morning."

Armel's Story

In a side room of the children's ward, Armel lay without moving, head encased in bandages, body wired up to machines. Kwayera sat by him, her face twisted with fear. All night long she had been there, huddled in an armchair, watching the changing luminous green dials and unable to sleep.

Miraculously the doctor who had examined Armel had spoken to her in French. He had told her that if there was any change in the situation, the nursing staff would contact him and he would come. This she found comforting, Armel was in good hands.

Towards morning, as she glanced at the silent face of her son, she thought she saw a minute flicker of his eyelids. Eagerly she pulled her chair closer to his bed, and gazed intently at his face. Another flicker, then another, like a light that is struggling with connection. Kwayera pressed the buzzer to summon the nurse.

"*Vous voyez?*" she cried, pointing at Armel.

"I'll call the doctor," said the nurse.

Neither of them knew what the other was saying, but they each understood the meaning behind the words.

Soon the doctor who spoke French arrived. After examining Armel and checking the machines, he told Kwayera that Armel was doing well. No doubt he would soon be fully conscious. He must have plenty of rest, she was not to worry him with questions about what had happened.

Kwayera nodded and settled down to wait.

❖　❖　❖

Papa wasn't there when Christophe woke up.

"He got a call from the hospital," Mbika said. "They wanted him to come and see a boy who was brought in yesterday."

Evidently Papa had not told his mother

about Christophe's fight with the Hutu boy, and she had no idea that it was Armel who was in hospital. Christophe felt sick with worry. Why had Papa been called to the hospital? Was Armel going to be all right? He struggled with his conscience, but he was unable to find the courage to tell his mother what was going on.

"You haven't eaten much breakfast," Mbika pointed out.

"I'm not hungry."

"How's your eye?"

"All right. I can see out of the other one."

"Are you going to be all right for school?"

"Yeah."

The last thing Christophe wanted was to stay at home. His mother would worry the truth out of him, he was sure, and there was no way he could face talking to her about what had happened.

When he arrived at school the others, like moths drawn to a light, were unable to keep their eyes away from his battered face.

"Armel's not at school today. Armel did it, didn't he?"

"I'm not telling."

They turned to Con. "Was it Armel?"

Con shrugged his shoulders.

Try as he might, Christophe was unable to stop thinking about Armel. He almost wished that he had stayed at home for the day.

◊ ◊ ◊

Armel returned to consciousness and the machines were taken away. His head still swathed in bandages, he lay in bed playing over his memory of the fight with the *inyenzi*. What exactly had happened? Foul play, it must have been foul play. What else could you expect from a cockroach?

He remembered seeing the creature scale a wall to get away from him, He had followed. After that he wasn't sure what had happened. He had been winning, he was sure of it, but now he was in hospital with a broken head. His knuckles were swollen and sore, which showed that he had landed some good punches. He had better not tell his mother that he had been fighting the cockroach. When he got out of hospital, he would finish off the fight.

True to her promise to the doctor, Kwayera did not question him about what had happened.

❖ ❖ ❖

"Nothing showed up on the tests that were done," the doctor told Kwayera. "If it carries on like this, Armel will soon be able to leave hospital."

"That's wonderful," cried Kwayera.

"If his friends hadn't managed to get an ambulance so quickly he might not have been so lucky."

"I must thank those children!" said Kwayera. Tears swelled up in her eyes.

A muscle quivered at the corner of the doctor's mouth, but Kwayera didn't notice. He said, "I'll come and see Armel tomorrow.

Take it easy, young man."

◇ ◇ ◇

"How is Armel?" Christophe asked his father that night.

"Making good progress."

"That's good," said Mbika.

Christophe shot a quick look at his mother. "Papa told you!"

"Of course he did," said Mbika. "And you should have told me too. Why didn't you?"

"I thought you'd be angry with me," said Christophe. His cheeks felt as if they were burning.

"I was," said Mbika, "But I'm not angry now."

◇ ◇ ◇

The next day when André arrived at his patient's bedside, Kwayera wasn't there. Her son was fast asleep, unaware of the doctor's presence. Sleep had closed his eyes and eased the lines of hatred from his face. He appeared young and innocent; he did not look like a young man who hated one of the boys in his class so much that he wanted to annihilate him.

This kid tried to kill my son, André thought. *And here am I, patching him up and sending him out into the world so that he can do it again. I've lost one son to the Hutus, I don't want to lose another. This boy's wounds are healing, but what about the lesions in his heart? How is it that a child like this can have so much hate in him? It's the poison of the past, it's a vicious circle of hate. Is there anything I could do which would help?*

André's heart felt like a dead weight in his chest. As he stood turning over his thoughts, his patient stirred and woke.

◇ ◇ ◇

Armel woke to find a man standing beside him. Fear shot through him: his mother wasn't there, the small side room was as silent as a tomb, he was helpless.

"Don't be afraid," the man said.

"I'm a doctor."

"You speak French?"

"I'm from the same part of the world as you are, I've come to tell you that the tests have shown nothing serious. You can almost certainly go back home tomorrow. But first I would like you to tell me what happened."

Armel looked deep into the doctor's eyes. He saw compassion and something more – understanding.

"I'm a Hutu," the doctor said softly.

"Are you? Then you'll understand!"

"I'd like to do so."

"They made me sit next to an *inyenzi* at school!" Armel felt a surge of hatred. "Can you imagine what that felt like? I walked out, but they made me go back. I changed places. I tried not to look at him, but I knew he was there! It made me feel sick, you understand?"

Tight-lipped, the doctor nodded.

Armel found a bitter taste in his mouth. He swallowed. He held out his hands. "Don't worry, I got him! I wasn't going to let him get away with it. I had to wait for a chance, and I got it! Look at my hands, I got him all right! We were fighting and I was going to win, then I woke up here with a sore head. I don't know what happened after that. I'll get him, see if I don't! He's not going to get away with it!"

"Get away with what?"

"With . . . with what they did." Armel could hardly get the words out. He could see the bodies piled up. He began to shiver. "He's a cockroach, isn't he?"

He felt a hand take hold of his, he heard the doctor say, "Tell me what happened," but the shivering wouldn't stop.

He and Laurent had come out of the forest, they had come back to the village. . .

"Take your time," the doctor said gently.

"They killed my baba," said Armel. Tears began to roll down his cheeks. "And my sisters. My mama was still alive. She had cuts, I thought she was dead."

He felt a gentle pressure on his hand. "Who killed them?" he heard the doctor say.

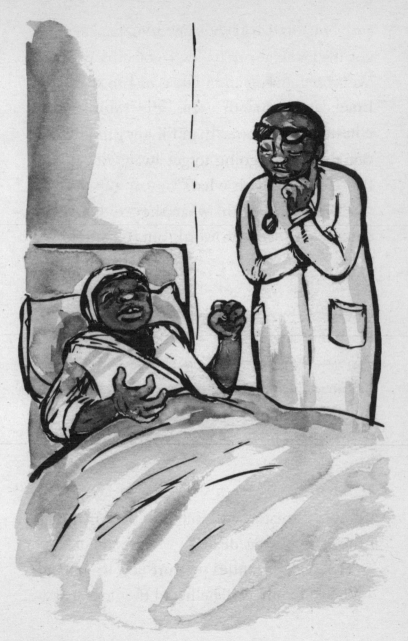

"The *inyenzi*. They came twice."

"Twice?"

"Once before the rains and again some time later," Armel said. His words were coming more quickly now, they were like caged creatures wanting to be let out. "The first time they came, we heard shouts and we ran into the forest. My sisters were scared, so was my mama. We had nothing to eat, no water. Next morning we crept back. They'd taken the goats, they'd taken what they wanted. There were bodies everywhere."

Armel felt bile rise into his mouth. He almost choked, but he cleared his throat. Baba had kept Mama and his sisters away from the bodies, but he had let Armel help.

"I dug holes for them," Armel said proudly. "I'm not a kid!"

The doctor's eyes were moist. They were full of a horror and sadness that met and mingled with Armel's own fear and misery. Armel knew he could say anything he wanted, and this doctor would listen. More than that, he would understand. Memories flooded into Armel's head, bad things, things he had been trying to forget. Once again he was shivering.

"What is it?" said the doctor quietly. He was still holding Armel's hand.

"They came back," Armel said. His voice began to break up. "There was no warning. Laurent and I were digging the land near the forest. We ran, we got away. But the others didn't. Next day we went back. They were lying in a heap."

Tears were rolling down Armel's cheeks. The doctor put out his hand and gently wiped them away.

"We . . . we dug holes," said Armel. "Mama was still alive. Laurent said I must take her to the *abazungu*, to the white people."

"Where was that?"

"Six days' journey. But it took longer than that. I had to carry her, she couldn't walk."

The nights had been the worst. Mama was hot and in pain. She was babbling strangely. Armel had been convinced that she was going to die. But the *abazungu* doctors had used their medicine to make Mama better. At first Armel was unnerved by the strange colour of their skins, but he had seen how kind they were and he had trusted them. They had sent Mama to a hospital and Armel had gone with her. Then they had sent the two of them to the UK.

"Where's your brother now?" asked the doctor.

"Laurent is fighting against the *inyenzi*,"

Armel said with pride. "He's going to pay them back. And I'm going to finish off the one I was fighting with, that's what I'm going to do when I get out of here. I don't know what happened, why I ended up here. He must have landed me one, that's what must have happened. He wanted to kill me."

"Then why did he call the ambulance?" asked the doctor.

"Call the ambulance?"

"You were fighting with the one you call the '*inyenzi*'," said the doctor. "You fell, you hit your head on a stone. You were out cold. The ... *inyenzi* ... didn't try to finish you off, as you put it. Nor did he run away. He was bruised and bleeding, he was shocked to see you lying so still. What did he do? He rang his friend and asked him to call an ambulance."

Silence filled the room, a silence broken only by the sound of footsteps echoing up and down the corridor. Armel was struggling with the doctor's words. The *inyenzi* had called for an ambulance? It made no sense. Why would an *inyenzi* have done that?

The doctor took out a handkerchief and wiped the sweat from his forehead. "Do you know what happened in Rwanda?"

"Of course I do! They did what they could to get rid of the cockroaches," cried Armel. "But they didn't finish off the job, and that's why we had to run away. If only they'd finished them all off, everything would have been all right."

"Let me tell you something," said the doctor. "The one you call a cockroach, the one you were fighting with, came from Rwanda. His little brother was killed by the Hutus. You hit your head on a stone and you were helpless. He could have finished you off. Then why didn't he? Why did he call an ambulance?"

Armel slowly shook his head.

"You don't have an answer, do you?" said the doctor. "Nor do I. There's something else I'd like you to know. Something that will surprise you."

Armel braced himself.

"Christophe is a Hutu, like you."

Startled, Armel burst out, "He can't be!"

"His father is a Hutu and his mother is a Tutsi."

"Surely not, surely you've made a mistake!"

"No mistake. Christophe is my son," said the doctor. "And I'm proud of him. I'll leave you now. You've got a lot to think about, young man. I'll see you again tomorrow before I discharge you."

Armel sank back on his pillows and closed his eyes.

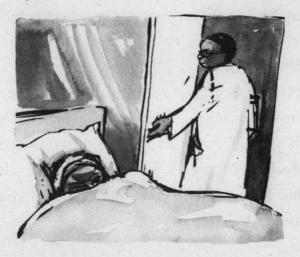

The Aftermath

"How's Armel?" Con asked as they walked back from school.

"A lot better," said Christophe. "My dad said it was lucky we got an ambulance so quickly. Armel could have died."

Papa had not exactly used those words, but Christophe was in no doubt that that was what Papa meant.

"Phew!"

"I wanted to run off, but I didn't," Christophe confessed with conscious pride.

"You couldn't have!" cried Con. He sounded shocked.

"No," agreed Christophe, though he knew very well that he easily might have done. "You know Armel?"

"Yeah?"

"His family got killed by Tutsis. That's what my dad said."

Con's eyes widened. "What for?"

"Because of what the Hutus did in my country. But you're not to talk about it and you mustn't tell anyone else at school. Promise?"

"Yeah."

"He's only got a mum."

They reached Con's house. "Coming in?" asked Con.

Christophe nodded. He fingered his eye — it was still a bit sore, but it was a lot better. Maybe he would see Kath; he had not seen her since his fight with Armel. Just as this thought was passing through his mind, Kath opened the door. She gave a smile that lit up her face, and she said, "Well, if it isn't Chris! Come in! Your eye looks a whole lot better!"

"Yeah," said Christophe, divided between delight and embarrassment that she had noticed him.

"Mam's taken the twins to get their booster shots. I'm to get you tea and there's some soda bread to go with it."

Con and Christophe threw their school bags on to the heap of shoes, scarves and fallen jackets that lay under the coat racks and followed Kath into the kitchen.

"And while I'm about it, you can tell me what's been going on. I never did get to the bottom of it," Kath said as she put the kettle on. "Con spun me a story about Who-twos and Two-twos, is that right?"

"Tutsis," said Christophe shyly.

"And the Who-twos started killing the Tootsis? And your little brother was killed, but you escaped? And you're a Who-two, but you look like a Tootsi?"

"That's right."

"And that's enough to make this kid try and murder you? Give over, isn't it time you all grew up?" Kath said impatiently. "My da was blown up by a bomb. And two of his brothers were murdered. And my mam's parents were killed, and her sister and the baby. That's why we're living over the water, to get away from it all. You can't go looking for revenge.

It poisons you."

"Poison?" said Christophe. "That's what my dad talks about. The poison from the past."

"He's right," said Kath. "Here now, here's your tea, Chris. Get a life, that's what I say."

As Christophe walked back home he thought about what Papa had told him. Bad things had happened in the Congo and now Armel and his mother were asylum-seekers, just as Christophe and his parents had been. Maybe one day Armel would tell him the story of what had happened, Papa had said. But then again, maybe Armel would prefer not to.

Christophe felt sorry for Armel. They were both Hutus, weren't they? And they had each wanted to hurt the other. What if they had succeeded? How would you feel if you knew that you had killed someone?

Christophe felt a shiver running up his back to think how nearly that had happened.

◇ ◇ ◇

A few days later, Christophe filed into the classroom behind Con and they sat down at their desks. He delved into his rucksack to find the books that he needed for the History lesson that was about to begin.

Con nudged him and hissed, "Look!"

Armel was sitting at his desk, taking out his books. Christophe felt a jolt of apprehension. Armel was back at school at last. Christophe could see a line on the back of Armel's head where the wound had healed. If only Armel would turn round! But the lesson was beginning and he had his eyes fixed on Miss Nagi.

"Do you think he's still got it in for you?" whispered Con.

"No talking, please," said Miss Nagi.

Christophe tried to concentrate on the lesson, but he found it hard. The lesson ended, they had to stay in their seats for the next one. Armel was talking to his neighbour and still his face was hidden.

Then it was time for the break.

Christophe half-rose, he wanted to go over to Armel, but something held him back. Between him and Armel were desks filled with kids scoffing and teasing and packing up their books. At that moment Armel stood up. He turned, and across the crowded room he gave Christophe a slow, shy smile.

Nicki Cornwell has previously worked as a social worker, a teacher, a university lecturer and an interpreter. She now divides her time between writing and painting and between London and Berry in France.

To visit Nicki Cornwell's website go to www.nickicornwell.com.